The Kilmory Coo

By Jill Jeffries

Matador
9 Priory Business Park
Kibworth Beauchamp
Leicestershire LE8 0RX, UK
Tel: (+44) 116 279 2299
Fax: (+44) 116 279 2277
Email: books@troubador.co.uk
Web: www.troubador.co.uk/matador

ISBN 978 1783060 917

British Library Cataloguing in Publication Data.
A catalogue record for this book is available from the British Library.

Matador is an imprint of Troubador Publishing Ltd

Very early one morning, The Kilmory Coo lay yawning in her field.

The sun was just starting to rise, the moon hadn't quite gone

to bed yet, and The Dougarie Dog was full of beans.

"Morning Coo!" yapped Dog. "You're a clever Coo,

and you know lots of things, don't you?"

"Well" said Coo smiling, "I like to think so."

"How do the sun and the moon know when to come out

and when to go in?"

Coo didn't know how the sun and the moon knew when to come out

and when to go in, but she didn't want to disappoint

The Dougarie Dog, so she thought it would be alright

to make something up.

Just this once.

3

"How?" said Coo, "Well, you know the moon is made of cheese?"

Dog stared at her in amazement.

"So, if they both came out at the same time

the heat of the sun would melt the cheesey moon right out

of the sky. All that melted cheese would make a terrible

mess of the fields,

so that's why the moon only comes out at night."

Dog's eyes were as big as saucers,

he *loved* cheese, so he dashed off in the direction

of the moon, hoping just a little bit might melt off

as the sun rose.

All this time, The Whiting Bay Worm had been quietly

hiding behind a weed, listening. Now Dog had gone,

he wanted to ask a question of his own.

"Coo!" he yelled, "Since you're so clever, could you tell me how

all the other animals grow up to be big, but I don't?

I've been very worried about it!"

Poor Coo didn't know that either, but she didn't want Worm

to worry, so she thought it would be alright

to make something up,

just this once more.

"You're very tiny so you can fit into your hole." Said Coo.

"If you were big you'd have nowhere to live."

Worm seemed very relieved to know there was a good reason

for his size, and Coo sighed with contentment.

News of the clever Coo, who could answer any question, quickly spread across Arran. Soon animals were queuing up to ask her even more things she didn't know the answers to.

"How do spiders make a web?" asked the hens.

"Spiders like to know where they've been, so they leave a trail behind them, but Spiders *always* get lost and end up going round in circles, so it turns into a web."

"How does it know when to rain?" honked Goose

"The farmer tells it when to." Guessed Coo.

"Well I wish he wouldn't tell it to so often!" muttered the sheep,

but The Corrie Crow interrupted by asking how clouds are made.

"Erm... all the little scraps of wool that the sheep leave on fences and gates get blown up into the sky, and they all get stuck together and stay there." said Coo desperately. She wasn't enjoying having to make up all these answers any more.

She didn't know how any of it happened, but she *really* didn't want to let anyone down, and she *really* didn't want to look stupid to her friends, so she just carried on making things up.

Eventually the animals ran out of questions, and Coo heaved a huge sigh of relief.

"Thank goodness that's over." She thought to herself.

But then she heard some murmuring amongst the sheep, and

one of them was shoved to the front.

"H-How does the water in the stream know which way to go?"

stammered the sheep, before jumping back behind her friends.

Tired, and running out of ideas, The Kilmory Coo dismissed

the question as quickly as she could.

"It doesn't." She said,

"Water is very stupid and it just follows the fish."

"Phew!" thought Coo. "I got away with it."

But then Crow said "Does it?

Let's go and look!"

Before Coo had a chance

to think, all the animals

started walking towards

Lagg burn.

Very reluctantly, Coo followed.

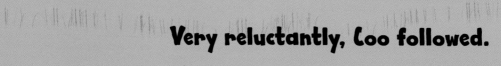

For a while they all watched the burn

flowing down the hill,

until one little fish,

then another,

then another,

swam *up* the burn,

the opposite way to the water.

"Oh dear" gulped Coo,

"Now I'm found out."

But the animals were all amazed.

"How can that be?" they asked, and they all turned round

to stare at The Kilmory Coo.

"Erm" stammered Coo, "Um, er, it's because..........."

But then she stopped,

and she thought,

and she simply said,

"I don't know how."

The animals were stunned for a moment,

but one by one, they started trying to work out how the water

really knew which way to go, and this made them happier

than *anything* Loo had said!

"Goodness!" Coo thought to herself. "Never again!

'I don't know' was the only sensible thing I said all day!"

THE END

Did you find the worm on every page?